CIP Data is available.
Published in the United States 2006 by
Blue Apple Books
P.O. Box 1380, Maplewood, N.J. 07040
www.blueapplebooks.com
Distributed in the U.S. by Chronicle Books
First Edition
Printed in China

ISBN 13: 978-1-59354-171-2
ISBN 10: 1-59354-171-6

1 3 5 7 9 10 8 6 4 2

Sylvie Jones

Go Back to Sleep

Pictures by Pascale Constantin

Blue Apple Books

This is the bedroom of
Willy John Jones.
In it he keeps
the toys that he owns.

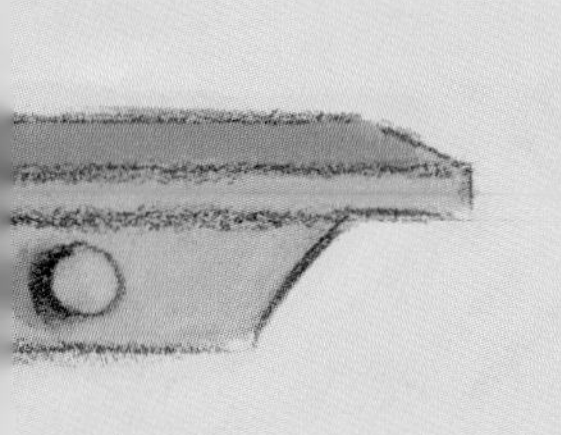

Willy was tired
and ready for bed.
His eyes felt sleepy.
So did his head!

To Bo Bear he said,
"No fooling around.
I want you to sleep.
Now don't make a sound."

3

Under the bed went Wheelie, a mouse,
where Willy's red slipper made her a warm house.

3

On top of the covers lay Charlie A. Sheep.
His eyes were closing. He wanted to sleep!

Near Willy's red cap Kitty rested his head.
He preferred lying there to Willy's big bed.

Willy had Sailor Monkey to protect him from harm.
For scaring monsters he worked like a charm.

Willy turned over and got comfy in bed.
He pulled the covers up over his head.

AND EVERYONE WENT TO SLEEP!

But not Bo Bear!

Bo Bear woke
Wheelie Mouse.
"Let's play,"
he whispered.

Wheelie Mouse
woke Charlie.

Charlie woke
Kitty.

Kitty woke
Sailor Monkey.

Wheelie Mouse squeaked.
Bo Bear grunted. Charlie baaa'd.
Kitty meowed. And Sailor Monkey said,
"Wind me. Wind me. Wind me up!"

"Go back to sleep! It's the middle of the night."
THE NOISE WOKE WILLY.

But no one listened.
Not even Wheelie Mouse.

So . . .

Willy put Bo Bear on the bed.

He put Wheelie Mouse next to him.

Willy put Charlie under the covers.

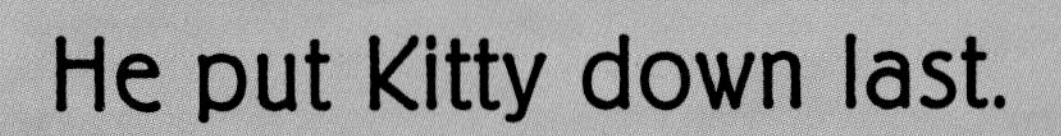

He put Kitty down last.

Willy picked up Sailor Monkey
and climbed into bed.
He pulled the covers
up over his head.

Good night, everyone!